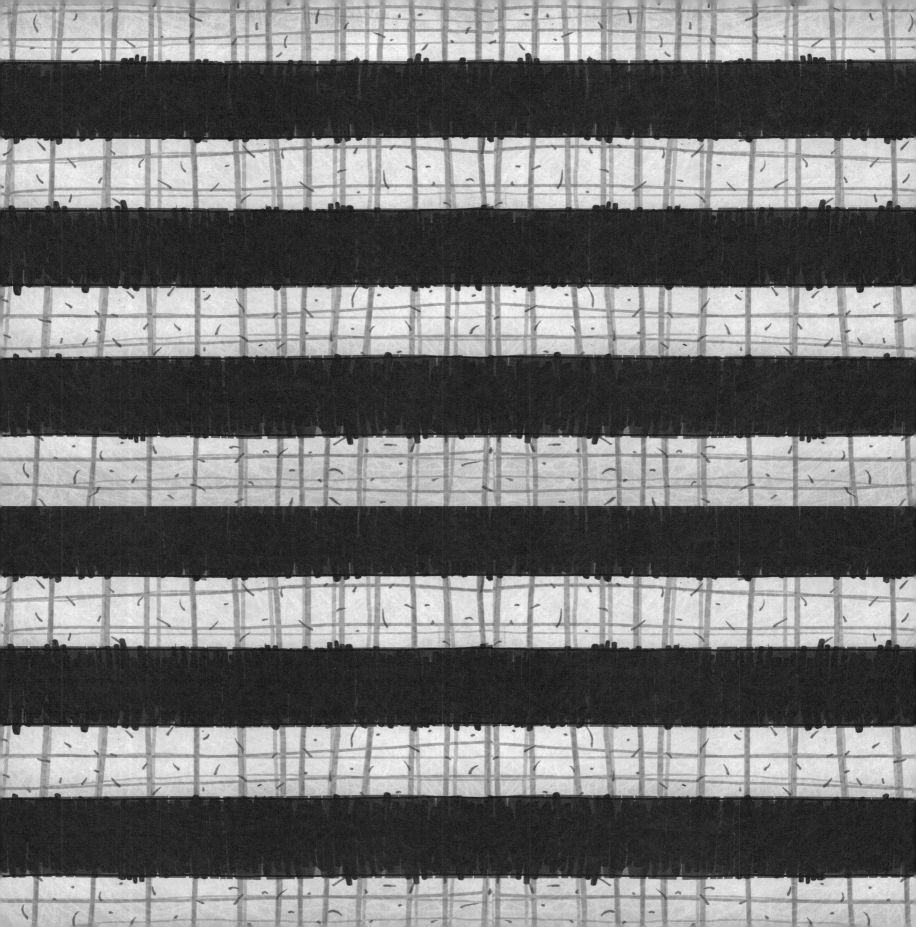

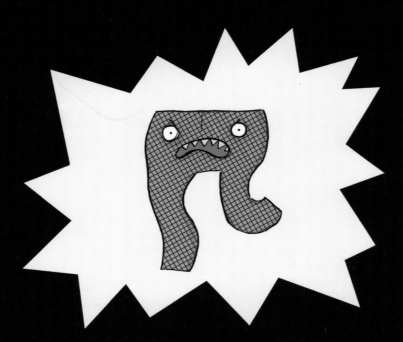

To Nathan, for putting up with me
when I am wearing my crabby pants. —jg

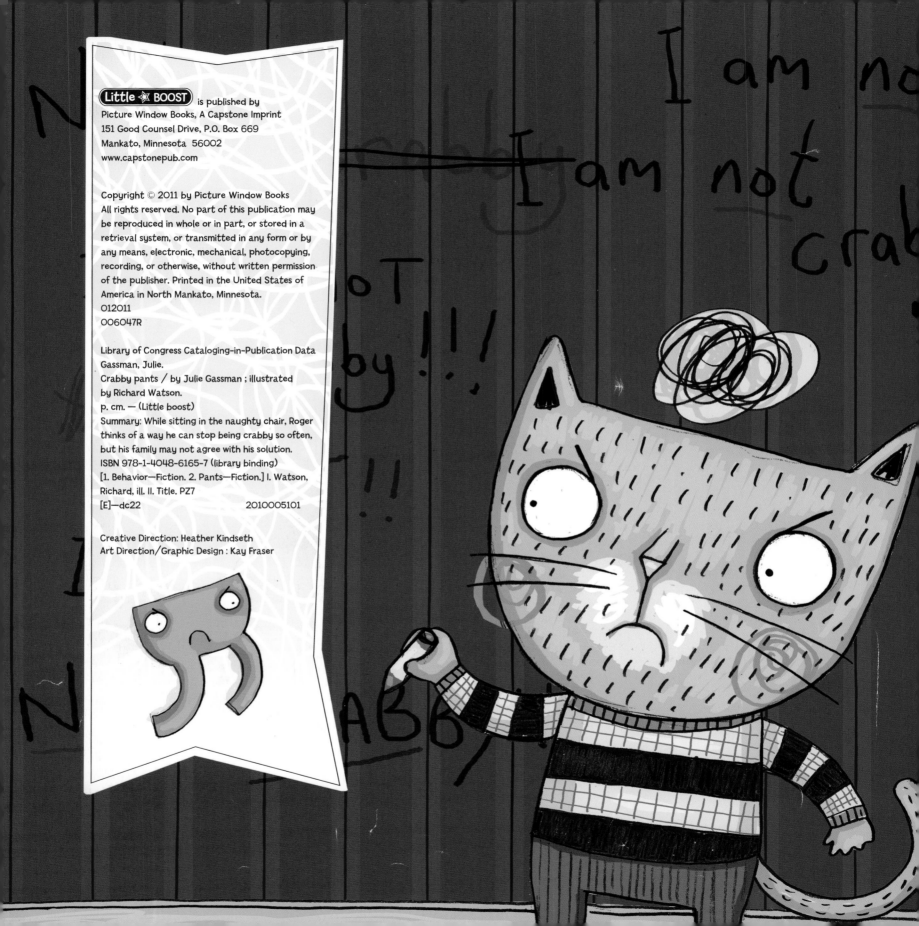

Little ⭐ BOOST is published by
Picture Window Books, A Capstone Imprint
151 Good Counsel Drive, P.O. Box 669
Mankato, Minnesota 56002
www.capstonepub.com

012011
006047R

Library of Congress Cataloging-in-Publication Data
Gassman, Julie.
Crabby pants / by Julie Gassman ; illustrated
by Richard Watson.
p. cm. — (Little boost)
Summary: While sitting in the naughty chair, Roger
thinks of a way he can stop being crabby so often,
but his family may not agree with his solution.
ISBN 978-1-4048-6165-7 (library binding)
[1. Behavior—Fiction. 2. Pants—Fiction.] I. Watson,
Richard, ill. II. Title. PZ7
[E]—dc22   2010005101

Creative Direction: Heather Kindseth
Art Direction/Graphic Design : Kay Fraser

Crabby Pants

by Julie Gassman   illustrated by Richard Watson

PICTURE WINDOW BOOKS
a capstone imprint

This is Roger.

He gets CRABBY.

A lot.

There was the morning his older brother
ate the last frozen waffle.

Roger was **stuck** eating cereal.

So Roger got CRABBY.

Then there was the day Roger's class
was supposed to go to the zoo.

"We cannot go to the zoo in a thunderstorm,"
his teacher said.

So Roger got CRABBY.

And what about the day he fell asleep waiting for his favorite TV show to come on?

His mom let him sleep through the
whole thing!

There was only one thing to do . . .

get CRABBY.

"You shouldn't be such a crabby pants,"
his older brother said.

That made Roger **even** CRABBIER.

Before he knew it,

Roger was sitting in the naughty chair.

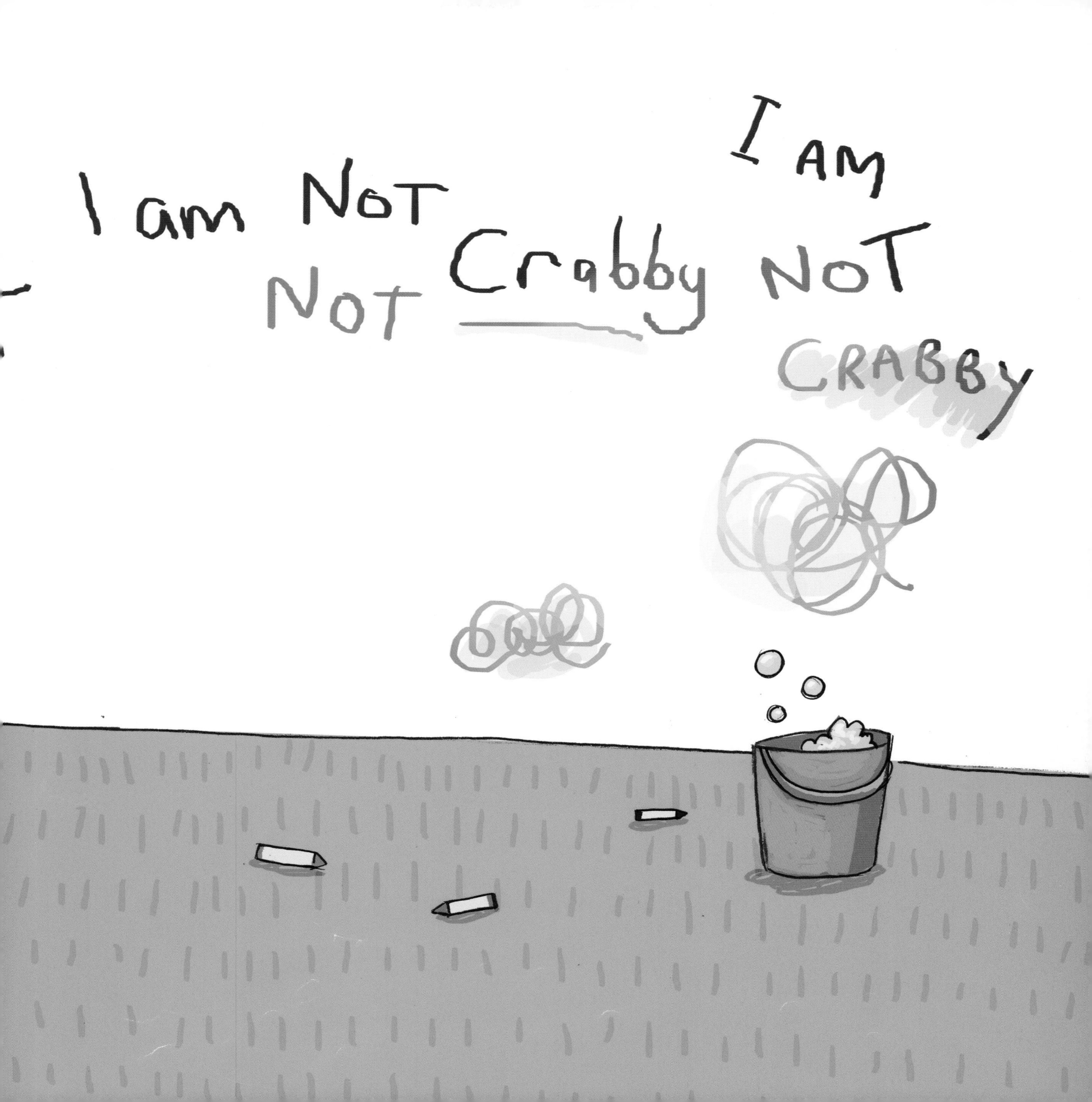
I am NOT
NOT
Crabby
I AM
NOT
CRABBY

Roger thought about what his brother had said.

Something CLICKED.

Roger thought of all the times he was crabby.

What did they all have in common?

His pants!

It was all clear now.

And Roger knew just what he had to do.

The next morning . . .

Roger showed his mom and dad how he had
solved his crabby problem.

"After all," said Roger,

"there's no such thing as

CRABBY

shorts."

Roger's mom and dad were not happy.

And soon, Roger was

CRABBY again.

That night . . .

Roger decided to take care of the CRABBY pants problem once and for all.

The next morning, Roger's family discovered what he had done.

"Isn't this great? Now, no one will ever get **CRABBY** again!" said Roger.

But he was
wrong.

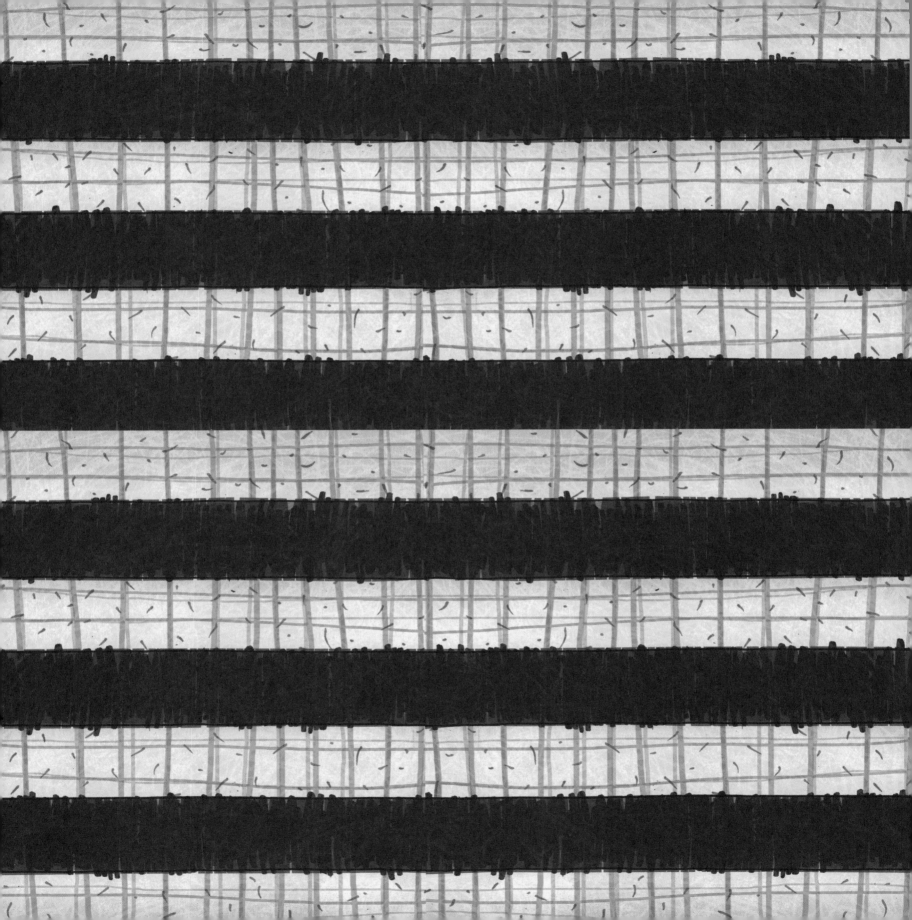

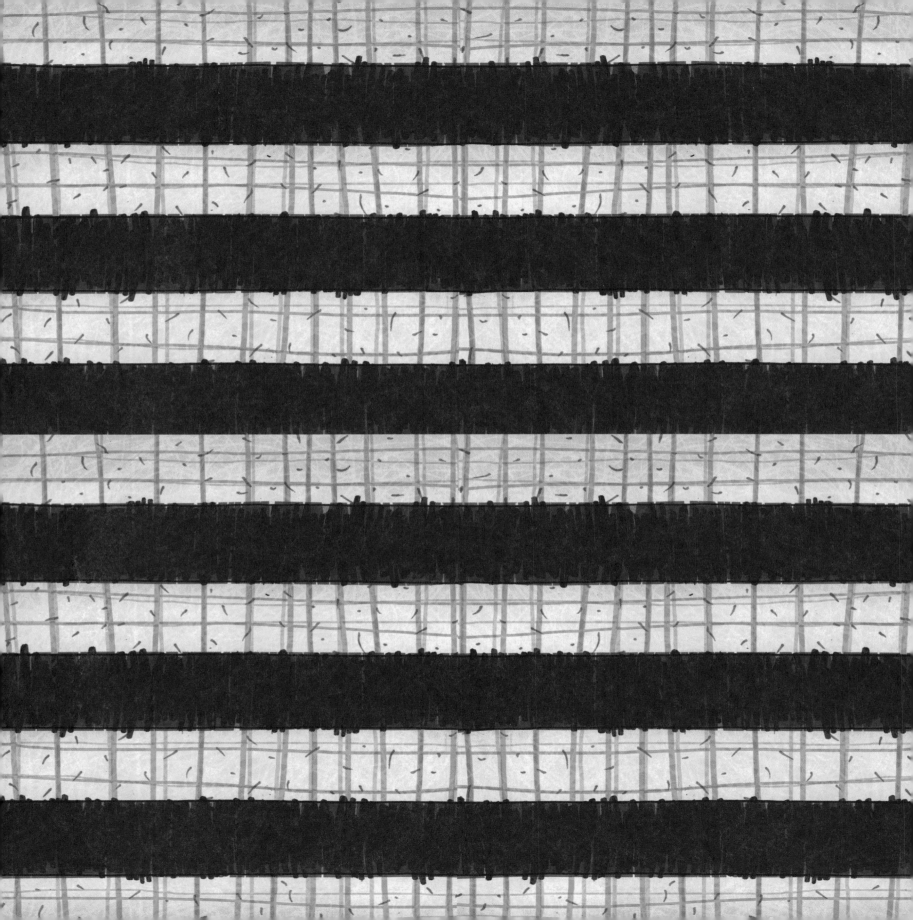